Date Due

For Anne and Jane

Maggee
and the Lake Minder

by Richard Thompson
illustrated by Eugenie Fernandes

Annick Press, Toronto, Canada

"I thought I heard singing," said Maggee looking in at the door.

"Oh, that was me," said the frog, "... and my friend. My name is Kawartha. And this is The Bird."

"I'm Maggee."

The Bird bobbed at Maggee, croaked once and tucked her head under her wing.

"Don't mind The Bird," said Kawartha. "She's not used to having company call. In fact, we've never had a child ever visit before. Lemonade?"

As he poured Maggee a glass he asked,

"Do you sing?"

"Oh yes," said Maggee. "I could sing, 'Row, Row, Row Your Boat.'"

"Very appropriate!" said the frog. "What better choice for a lakeside serenade."

"It's not a lake in the song, it's a stream," croaked The Bird. She dipped her beak into her lemonade and made a sour face.

"That's no problem," said Maggee. "I'll just change it to lake."

"Wouldn't rhyme then," muttered The Bird. "...merrily across the lake...life is but a cake.... Ridiculous."

"We'll love it," declared the frog.

When Maggee had finished, the frog clapped his small webby hands and his big webby feet together with great slapping noises. The Bird rumpled her feathers and stared unblinking with her tiny black eyes.

"Now you sing," Maggee told the frog.

Kawartha cleared his throat and sang a deep green rendition of "Froggie Went A-courting." He bowed when he was done, and Maggee clapped.

"I know!" she said. "Let's have a talent show! The table can be the stage. Do you want to be in our show, The Bird?"

"No!" croaked The Bird.

"You go first then, Kawartha."

The frog stood on the table and recited a poem.

Then Maggee showed off her pliers, sauts and entrechats.

"Bravo," cried Kawartha. "More! More!"

"Enough," croaked The Bird.

"More!" cried Maggee.

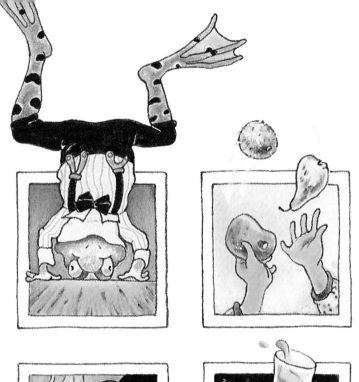

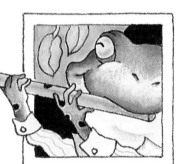

So Kawartha did this.
And Maggee did this.
"Excellent!" declared
Kawartha. "More! More!"
"More than enough,"
croaked The Bird.

"Your turn, Kawartha," said
Maggee.
So Kawartha did this.

And Maggee did this.

"Magnificent!" shouted Kawartha. "More! More!"
"Too much," croaked The Bird. And out the window
she flew.

"Doesn't The Bird like our show?" said Maggee.

"Of course, she does," said Kawartha.

"Listen to this," said Maggee.

Maggee repeated, "She sells sea shells down by the sea shore" really fast six times without making a mistake.

"Incredible!" said Kawartha. "Watch this,"

He astounded Maggee by catching invisible golf balls in a paper bag.

"That's astounding," said Maggee. "Let's sing one song together, and then I have to go."

They sang a slow song so it would last, but eventually even slow songs come to an end and it was time for Maggee to go.

"Before you do, though," said Kawartha, "I want to give you a present." He jumped off the table—SPLASH—and waded out the door.

"Splash?" said Maggee. She looked over the edge of the table. The floor was covered in water! "What's going on?" said Maggee.

"The drain's plugged." The Bird was perched on the window sill.

"I beg your pardon?" said Maggee.

"The drain's plugged," said The Bird. "That silly frog has forgotten about checking the drain."

"What do you mean?" asked Maggee.

"That's his job," said The Bird. "He's a Lake Minder, and it's his job to mind that the water comes in and goes out."

"What's going to happen?" asked Maggee in alarm. "Is the lake going to flood?"

"Of course, it's going to flood," croaked The Bird. "What do you expect?"

"This is terrible," cried Maggee, "and it's my fault."

The Bird hopped from the window sill onto the table.

"No, it is not your fault," she said. "You are not Kawartha. Come with me, and we'll see what we can do."

She long-legged out the door, and Maggee waded after her.

The Bird led her along the lake to the drain hole.

"Clogged!" croaked The Bird. "Rocks and tree bits, roots and muddles of weeds... It'll be a job clearing that out!"

"I'll help," said Maggee. "We can do it!"

It WAS a job, but eventually the bird and the girl, working together, managed to get most of the tangle cleared away.

"Alright," said The Bird. "I'll just move this rock and....AAAIIIIIIEEE!"

Suddenly, the water began funnelling down the drain swirling and hissing and it was sucking down The Bird, too.

"AAAIIEEEE! Help!"

Maggee clutched a twisty root in one hand and grabbed The Bird by one wing with the other. She held on tight until the last of the flood slurped away down the hole.

Bedraggled and muddy and shivering cold, Maggee and The Bird squelched back to Kawartha's house. The Bird made them a cup of hot chocolate to warm them.

"Would you like me to sing you one of my songs?" croaked The Bird shyly.

"That would be terrific!" said Maggee.

But right at that moment, Kawartha flip-flopped into the room.

"Here you are," he announced. "A lovely bouquet of marsh lilies . . . Oh, my goodness, what happened to you?"

"While you were paddling about in the weeds, we were unplugging the drain," croaked The Bird.

"Unplugging the drain?" said the frog, blinking his big round eyes.

"And The Bird almost got sucked down," said Maggee.

"Oh dear," said the frog slumping into a chair. "I quite forgot about the drain . . ."

"And about getting supper ready," said The Bird. "And about trimming the reeds, and . . ."

"I'm very sorry," said Kawartha. "But I was having so much fun . . ."

"Fun is for fishes, my friend," said The Bird. "You are a Kawartha, a Lake Minder . . ."

Maggee stood up.

"I have to go home," she said. "I'm sorry I caused so much trouble, The Bird."

"Not you!" croaked The Bird.

Kawartha jumped up and pushed the bouquet of marsh lilies into Maggee's arms.

"Will you come again?" he asked.

"I don't think I should," said Maggee.

"Oh please!" cried Kawartha. "Just one song and a cup of tea, and then right back to work. I promise. Do come back. Please."

Maggee looked at The Bird.

"Yes, do," said The Bird.

"And you can sing your song," said Maggee.

"She dances beautifully as well!" said Kawartha.

Maggee did come back—all summer long. And
Kawartha always remembered to mind the lake.

Annick Press gratefully acknowledges the support of The Canada Council and the Ontario Arts Council.

Canadian Cataloguing in Publication Data

Thompson, Richard, 1951–
  Maggee and the lake minder

ISBN 1-55037-154-1 (bound)   ISBN 1-55037-152-5 (pbk.)

I. Fernandes, Eugenie, 1943–   .   II. Title

PS8589.H65M34 1991   jC813'.54   C90-095575-9
PZ7.T46Ma   1991

The art in this book was rendered in water colour, pen, and water colour pencils. The type was set in Oracle II, by Attic Typesetting Inc.

Distribution for Canada and The USA:

Firefly Books Ltd.,
250 Sparks Avenue
North York, Ontario   M2H 2S4

Printed and bound in Canada
by D.W. Friesen & Sons
∞ Printed on Acid-Free Paper